Dandelion Launchers

Reading and Writing Activities
for Units 8-10

PhonicBooks™

www.phonicbooks.co.uk   Enquiries@phonicbooks.co.uk
Tel: 07711 963355   Fax: 01666 823 411

Contents

Notes on Dandelion Launchers Workbooks

Dandelion Launchers Workbooks contain a variety of multisensory activities and games linked to the stories in the Dandelion Launchers reading scheme. The activities are designed to help develop the skills underlying fluency in reading and writing.

To become a reader, a learner needs to acquire the skill of pushing together individual sounds to make a word. This process is referred to as 'blending'.

To spell words accurately, a learner needs to be able to break a word up into its component sounds. This process is called 'segmenting'. The learner can then write the letters that represent the sounds in a word.

The activities offered will develop blending and segmenting skills in a fun and accessible way for the younger child.

The workbooks also include activities for letter formation, developing expressive vocabulary through retelling the stories and first comprehension exercises.

Clear instructions for every activity appear at the bottom of each page.

Dandelion Launchers Workbook Units 8-10

Dandelion Launchers Workbook Units 8-10 is divided into three units or levels. Each unit is based on four reading books from the corresponding unit in the reading scheme.

Books in Units 8-10 extend children's reading into decoding four-sound and five-sound words with adjacent consonants.

Units 8 and 9 cover the transition from cvc (consonant/vowel/consonant) words to words with adjacent consonants with three and four sounds.

Unit 8 continues to work on cvc words while also introducing words with a cvcc structure such as 'jump'. Books in Unit 9 continue this systematic progression by introducing words with a ccvc structure such as 'pram'.

The progression to reading four-sound words is a huge leap for some children so this workbook provides lots of activities to reinforce and support blending and segmenting words at this level.

Books in Unit 10 continue this steady progression by introducing ccvcc words with five sounds such as 'stunt'.

Some of the activities in the pack can be done before reading the books and others after reading them. This systematic approach helps the readers to enjoy success at each stage and will motivate them to continue learning.

Each activity has instructions at the bottom of the page to ensure understanding.

The progression in this workbook is as follows:

> Unit 8:   cvc* and cvcc words
>
> Unit 9:   ccvc words
>
> Unit 10:   ccvcc words

*c = consonant
v = vowel

Planning your lessons

These suggestions will help parents and teachers use the activities in this pack to reinforce and support reading development.

1. The lesson should be offered daily, when possible, and not last more than 15 minutes initially with younger children.

2. The activities in this pack support the important transition from reading words with three sounds (cvc words such as 'dog') to reading longer words with four and then five sounds with adjacent consonants, such as 'hand' and 'crisp'. Some children may find the transition to reading and spelling words with four and then five sounds more challenging. This is a normal part of reading development. This pack provides a variety of activities to support this important stage of learning.

3. Model segmenting words into sounds, and blending sounds into words orally. Encourage the reader to point to the spellings (graphemes) as they sound out the words. Make sure that the reader is matching the sounds in the words to the spellings on the page when reading and spelling. If the reader is missing sounds, indicate where this has occurred in the word.

4. Try to make the lessons as fun as possible, using the games in the pack to reinforce and support new learning.

5. Always ask the child to say the sounds and push them together to read new words when playing a game. The teacher or parent should model this for the child and do the same when playing.

6. Continue to reinforce the appropriate use of capital letters. Draw children's attention to them where they are used in the activities. Encourage them to find capital letters in books, comics and signs when reading.

Some tips for your lessons

- Lessons should be exciting and fun.

- Give plenty of praise and encouragement.

- Provide small amounts of new learning in each lesson.

- Provide lots of opportunity for rehearsal.

- Make lessons as multisensory as possible, involving the senses of touch, sight and speech.

- Hand success back to the child. If a child reads a word incorrectly, provide them with the missing information so that they can blend the sounds and read the word themselves.

- Use letter sounds, not names.

- Make sure you do not add extra sounds to a sound i.e. 'm' 'a' 't' and not 'muh' 'ah' 'tuh'.

- Encourage the learner to sound out words when reading, writing and playing games.

- Use games as a way to provide needed rehearsal of new learning. Each one of our books has a game at the back which can be photocopied.

Dandelion Launchers

This book belongs to

PhonicBooks™

www.phonicbooks.co.uk   Enquiries@phonicbooks.co.uk
Tel: 07711 963355   Fax: 01666 823 411

Dandelion Launchers tick chart
Units 8-10

Unit 8 'Lost'

Unit 9 'Bob is Glum'

Unit 10 'Stunt Rat'

Reading and Writing Activities

Unit 8

Initial missing sound

___ a n d

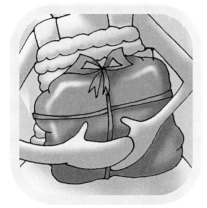

___ i f t

___ e n t

___ u m p

Fill in the missing sounds. Can be offered as a written activity or using the cut-out squares below.

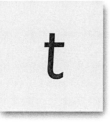

t   j   h   g

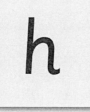

Second missing sound

l ___ m p

t ___ n k

c ___ t s

t ___ n t

Fill in the missing sounds. Can be offered as a written activity or using the cut-out squares below.

a   a   e   a

Third missing sound

j   u   p

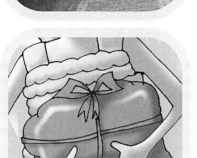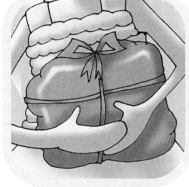

g   i   t

h   a   d

l   a   p

Fill in the missing sounds. Can be offered as a written activity or using the cut-out squares below.

n   m   f   m

Fourth missing sound

c a t __

t e n __

h a n __

t a n __

Fill in the missing sounds. Can be offered as a written activity or using the cut-out squares below.

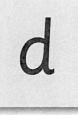 d   k   s   t

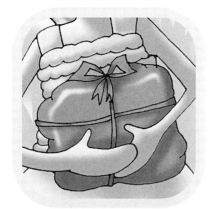

Initial and third missing sounds

i   t

a   p

u   p

a   s

Fill in the missing sounds. Can be offered as a written activity or using the cut-out squares below.

f   j   c   m   l   m   g   t

Second and last missing sounds

t _ _ n _ _

t _ _ n _

c _ _ t _

h _ _ n _

Fill in the missing sounds. Can be offered as a written activity or using the cut-out squares below.

t	a	d	a	s	e	k	a

All missing sounds

Fill in the missing sounds.

Book 8a - Retell the story

'Lost'

This page can be photocopied onto card. Cut out these pictures for retelling the story or for children to make their own story. Can also be used to reinforce vocabulary.

Book 8a - Comprehension

"Help! Sam is lost!"

"Mum!" said Sam,
"You got lost!"

"I will just pop in,"
said Mum.

Mum and Sam went to
the bank.

Cut out the sentences. Read and match to the correct pictures.

Book 8a - Sentence dictation

_____   _____   _____   _____   _____   _____   _____   _____   _____

_____   _____   _____   to   the   _____   _____   _____.

Offer the sentence below as dictation. Encourage the children to sound out the words as they spell them.

Mum and Sam went to the bank.

Word handwriting

Book 8a - Sentence handwriting

Mum and Sam

went to the bank.

Mum ran up the

ramp to get Sam.

Handwriting practice for the key words for Book 8a.

Book 8a - Free writing

Free writing with picture cues. This page can also be used for sentence dictation using sentences from the book.

High-frequency words: to, the, I, said, a, is, you

Book 8b - Retell the story

'Jump!'

This page can be photocopied onto card. Cut out these pictures for retelling the story or for children to make their own story. Can also be used to reinforce vocabulary.

Book 8b - Comprehension

Bob can land on
the mat.

"I will end up with a
limp."

"Let's jump off the
bunk bed."

Viv has to lift Meg
off the bed.

Cut out the sentences. Read and match to the correct pictures.

Book 8b - Sentence dictation

"I _____ _____ _____

with   a   _____."

Offer the sentence below as dictation. Encourage the children to sound out the words as they spell them.

"I will end up with a limp."

Book 8b - Sentence handwriting

Let's jump off the
bunk bed.

Viv has to lift
Meg off the bed.

Handwriting practice for the key words for Book 8b.

Book 8b - Free writing

Free writing with picture cues. This page can also be used for sentence dictation using sentences from the book.

High-frequency words: to, the, I, with, a, has

Book 8c - Retell the story

'Junk'

This page can be photocopied onto card. Cut out these pictures for retelling the story or for children to make their own story. Can also be used to reinforce vocabulary.

Book 8c - Comprehension

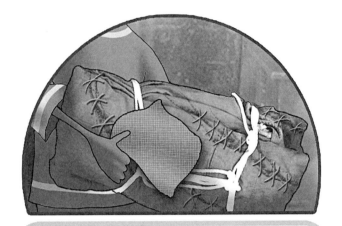

Alf met Hank at the dump.

"I can mend that old tent," said Hank.

Hank and Alf went off to camp.

"I must get rid of this old tent," said Alf.

Cut out the sentences. Read and match to the correct pictures.

Book 8c - Sentence dictation

"I

of   this   old   ."

Offer the sentence below as dictation. Encourage the children to sound out
the words as they spell them.

"I must get rid of this old tent."

Book 8c - Sentence handwriting

Hank and Alf
went off to camp.

"I can mend that
old tent," said
Hank.

Handwriting practice for the key words for Book 8c.

Book 8c - Free writing

Free writing with picture cues. This page can also be used for sentence dictation using sentences from the book.

High-frequency words: I, of, this, old, said, to, the, that

Book 8d - Retell the story

'The Gift'

This page can be photocopied onto card. Cut out these pictures for retelling the story or for children to make their own story. Can also be used to reinforce vocabulary.

Book 8d - Comprehension

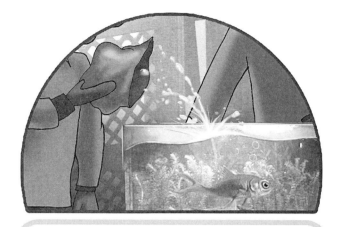

Alf got a gift from his Dad.

"It is the best gift!" said Alf.

Alf felt the gift with his hand.

"Can I give you a hint?" said Dad.

Cut out the sentences. Read and match to the correct pictures.

Book 8d - Sentence dictation

a

_____ _____ _____   _____ _____ _____   a   _____ _____ _____ _____

from   his   _____ .

Offer the sentence below as dictation. Encourage the children to sound out the words as they spell them.

Alf got a gift from his Dad.

Book 8d - Sentence handwriting

Alf felt the gift
with his hand.

"Can I give you a
hint?" said Dad.

Handwriting practice for the key words for Book 8d.

Book 8d - Free writing

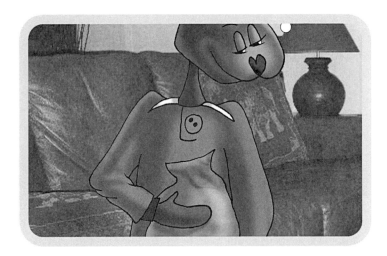

Free writing with picture cues. This page can also be used for sentence dictation using sentences from the book.

High-frequency words: a, from, his, the, with, is, cold, said, I, give, you, live

Spelling list

lost

hand

help

list

lump

mend

land

wind

sand

went

A list of words from this Unit to be used for spelling practice.

Unit 8 - Game : vcc, cvcc

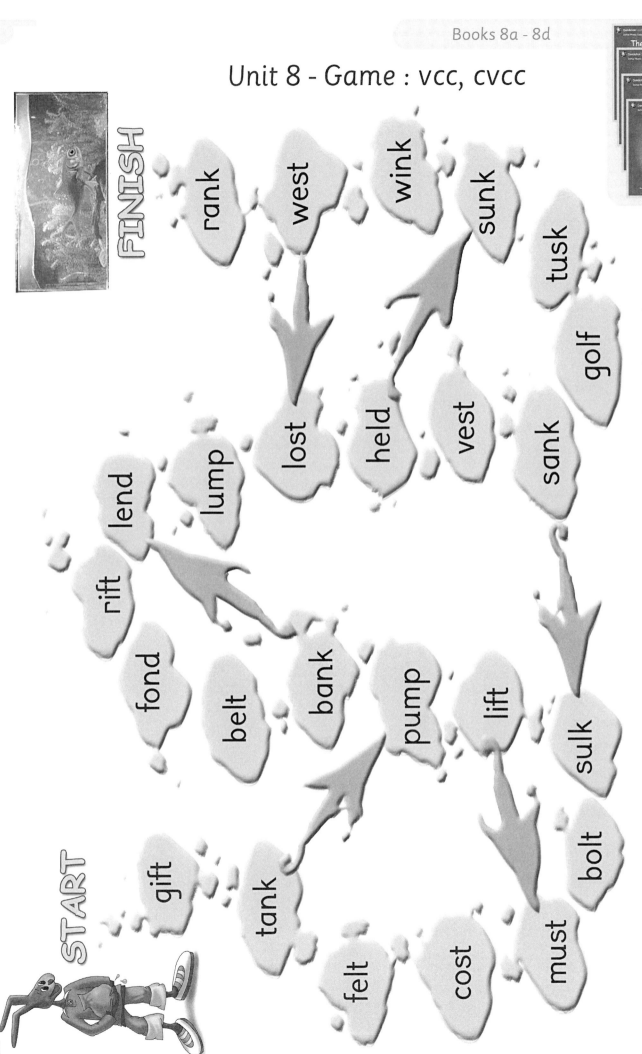

FINISH

START

rank

west

wink

sunk

tusk

golf

lost

held

vest

sank

lend

lump

rift

fond

bank

belt

pump

lift

sulk

gift

tank

felt

cost

must

bolt

The Gift

Junk

Jump!

Lost

This game is for 1-4 players. Play with counters and die. Players take turns to throw the dice and move their counter. Children read the word aloud as they land on it. Make sure the children use sounds rather than letter names.

40

Reading and Writing Activities
Unit 9

Initial missing sound

_ w i g

_ r a m

_ p o t

_ l u m

Fill in the missing sounds. Can be offered as a written activity or using the cut-out squares below.

g   s   p   t

Second missing sound

f _ a n

g _ a n

f _ a g

s _ i p

Fill in the missing sounds. Can be offered as a written activity or using the cut-out squares below.

r   n   l   l

Third missing sound

g l ___ m

s p ___ t

p r ___ m

f l ___ n

Fill in the missing sounds. Can be offered as a written activity or using the cut-out squares below.

a   u   a   o

Fourth missing sound

g r a ___

s n i ___

t w i ___

s p o ___

Fill in the missing sounds. Can be offered as a written activity or using the cut-out squares below.

g   n   t   p

Initial and third missing sounds

_ r _ m

_ p _ t

_ w _ g

_ l _ g

Fill in the missing sounds. Can be offered as a written activity or using the cut-out squares below.

a	t	a	s	o	f	i	p

Second and last missing sounds

s _ o _

s _ i _

f _ a _

p _ a _

Fill in the missing sounds. Can be offered as a written activity or using the cut-out squares below.

t n p l p r m n

All missing sounds

Fill in the missing sounds.

Book 9a - Retell the story

'Bob is Glum'

This page can be photocopied onto card. Cut out these pictures for retelling the story or for children to make their own story. Can also be used to reinforce vocabulary.

Book 9a - Comprehension

A spud from Gran.

Bob got milk from Viv.

Bob can not fit in
the cat flap.

Bob got ham from
Mum.

Cut out the sentences. Read and match to the correct pictures.

Book 9a - Sentence dictation

___ ___ ___ ___ ___ ___

___ the ___ ___ ___ .

Offer the sentence below as dictation. Encourage the children to sound out the words as they spell them.

Bob can not fit in the cat flap.

Word handwriting

Book 9a - Sentence handwriting

Dad got him a

bit of flan.

Bob can not fit in

the cat flap.

Handwriting practice for the key words for Book 9a.

Book 9a - Free writing

Free writing with picture cues. This page can also be used for sentence dictation using sentences from the book.

High-frequency words: a, of, his, he, the

Book 9b - Retell the story

'Don't Spill!'

This page can be photocopied onto card. Cut out these pictures for retelling the story or for children to make their own story. Can also be used to reinforce vocabulary.

Book 9b - Comprehension

Viv fills the cups to
the brim.

Viv and Fred trip and
spill the milk.

Meg laps up the milk
from the rug.

"Yes but don't spill it!"
says Mum.

Cut out the sentences. Read and match to the correct pictures.

Book 9b - Sentence dictation

the

_____ _____ _____

to   the   _____ _____ _____ _____ .

Offer the sentence below as dictation. Encourage the children to sound out the words as they spell them.

Viv fills the cups to the brim.

Book 9b - Sentence handwriting

Viv fills the cups
to the brim.

Meg laps up the
milk from the rug.

Handwriting practice for the key words for Book 9b.

Book 9b - Free writing

Free writing with picture cues. This page can also be used for sentence dictation using sentences from the book.

High-frequency words: we, have, a, of, don't, says, the, to, is

Book 9c - Retell the story

'Floss'

This page can be photocopied onto card. Cut out these pictures for retelling the story or for children to make their own story. Can also be used to reinforce vocabulary.

Book 9c - Comprehension

Gran is glad to have Floss.

Snip, snip! Trim, trim!

Gran got Floss in the tub.

"Floss was left in the dump," said the vet.

Cut out the sentences. Read and match to the correct pictures.

Book 9c - Sentence dictation

is

to   have   .

Offer the sentence below as dictation. Encourage the children to sound out the words as they spell them.

Gran is glad to have Floss.

Book 9c - Sentence handwriting

Gran is glad to have Floss.

"Floss was left in the dump," said the vet.

Handwriting practice for the key words for Book 9c.

Book 9c - Free writing

Free writing with picture cues. This page can also be used for sentence dictation using sentences from the book.

High-frequency words: was, the, said, I, to, have

Book 9d - Retell the story

'Stop the Pram!'

This page can be photocopied onto card. Cut out these pictures for retelling the story or for children to make their own story. Can also be used to reinforce vocabulary.

Book 9d - Comprehension

Jill runs with the pram.
Jill trips.

Rex runs to grab the pram.

Ted bumps in the pram.

Rex has skill. He gets Ted from the pram!

Cut out the sentences. Read and match to the correct pictures.

Book 9d - Sentence dictation

The _____ _____

_____ , _____ .

Offer the sentence below as dictation. Encourage the children to sound out the words as they spell them.

The pram went bump, bump.

Book 9d - Sentence handwriting

Jill, the doll, gets

Ted in the pram.

The pram bumps

on the steps.

Handwriting practice for the key words for Book 9d.

Book 9d - Free writing

Free writing with picture cues. This page can also be used for sentence dictation using sentences from the book.

High-frequency words: the, with, to, has, he

Spelling list

flap

pram

stop

grub

step

glum

grab

snip

blob

flip

A list of words from this Unit to be used for spelling practice.

Unit 9 - Game : ccvc

FINISH

START

Stop the Pram!

Floss

Don't Spill!

Bob is Glum

fluff
stop
skip
spell
slam
plug
stag
trek
skid
trot
flop
stuff
grin
sled
swam
glum
frog
grim
fled
clap
dress
drip
stop
drum
crab

This game is for 1-4 players. Play with counters and die. Players take turns to throw the dice and move their counter. Children read the word aloud as they land on it. Make sure the children use sounds rather than letter names.

Reading and Writing Activities
Unit 10

Initial missing sound

_ r i s p

_ l u m s

_ r o g s

_ t u m p

Fill in the missing sounds. Can be offered as a written activity or using the cut-out squares below.

s	c	p	f

Second missing sound

s _ i p s

f _ a g s

p _ a n k

s _ u n k

Fill in the missing sounds. Can be offered as a written activity or using the cut-out squares below.

l   k   k   l

Third missing sound

f r ___ g s

s k ___ n k

c r ___ s p

p l ___ m s

Fill in the missing sounds. Can be offered as a written activity or using the cut-out squares below.

u   o   u   i

Fourth missing sound

p l a __ k

s k i __ s

s t u __ p

c r i __ p

Fill in the missing sounds. Can be offered as a written activity or using the cut-out squares below.

m   s   n   p

Fifth missing sound

p l u m

s k u n

s t u m

f r o g

Fill in the missing sounds. Can be offered as a written activity or using the cut-out squares below.

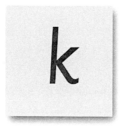

k   s   s   p

Initial and third missing sounds

_ l _ g s

_ r _ s p

_ l _ m s

_ l _ n k

Fill in the missing sounds. Can be offered as a written activity or using the cut-out squares below.

c u a p p f i a

Second and fourth missing sounds

p   u   s

s   u   k

p   a   k

f   o   s

Fill in the missing sounds. Can be offered as a written activity or using the cut-out squares below.

l   g   l   k   n   r   m   n

All missing sounds

Fill in the missing sounds.

Book 10a - Retell the story

'Stunt Rat'

This page can be photocopied onto card. Cut out these pictures for retelling the story or for children to make their own story. Can also be used to reinforce vocabulary.

Book 10a - Comprehension

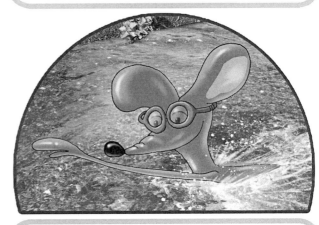

Ken swims in the pond.

Ken lifts up the twigs.

Ken sprints off and Bob pants.

Ken jumps and skips.

Cut out the sentences. Read and match to the correct pictures.

Book 10a - Sentence dictation

Offer the sentence below as dictation. Encourage the children to sound out the words as they spell them.

Ken sprints off and Bob pants.

Word handwriting

stunt

crisp

slept

plums

Book 10a - Sentence handwriting

Ken swims in the

pond.

Ken sprints off

and Bob pants.

Handwriting practice for the key words for Book 10a.

Book 10a - Free writing

Free writing with picture cues. This page can also be used for sentence dictation using sentences from the book.

High-frequency words: is, he, as, I, be, a, says, the

Book 10b - Retell the story

'Punk Smells Crisps'

This page can be photocopied onto card. Cut out these pictures for retelling the story or for children to make their own story. Can also be used to reinforce vocabulary.

Book 10b - Comprehension

Punk trots on.
He smells ham.

Punk stands and sniffs.

Punk, the skunk, sniffs the sand.

"I can smell a crust ..."

Cut out the sentences. Read and match to the correct pictures.

Book 10b - Sentence dictation

the

.

Offer the sentence below as dictation. Encourage the children to sound out the words as they spell them.

Punk lifts the lid and jumps in.

Book 10b - Sentence handwriting

Punk, the skunk, sniffs the sand.

Punk lifts the lid and jumps in.

Handwriting practice for the key words for Book 10b.

Book 10b - Free writing

Free writing with picture cues. This page can also be used for sentence dictation using sentences from the book.

High-frequency words: the, he, I, a

Book 10c - Retell the story

'Frank Swims'

This page can be photocopied onto card. Cut out these pictures for retelling the story or for children to make their own story. Can also be used to reinforce vocabulary.

Book 10c - Comprehension

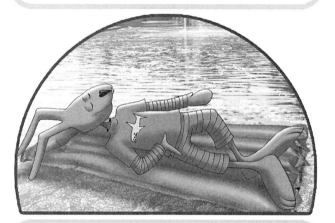

Alf jumps on. Frank
flips off in to the pond.

Frank and Alf slept
in the tents.

Alf helps him stand up.
Frank grunts.

Frank rests in the pond.
It is bliss.

Cut out the sentences. Read and match to the correct pictures.

Book 10c - Sentence dictation

to   the

_____ _____

for   a   _____ .

Offer the sentence below as dictation. Encourage the children to sound out
the words as they spell them.

Frank limps to the pond for a swim.

Book 10c - Sentence handwriting

Frank and Alf
slept in the tents.

Frank swims and
rests in the pond.
It is bliss.

Handwriting practice for the key words for Book 10c.

Book 10c - Free writing

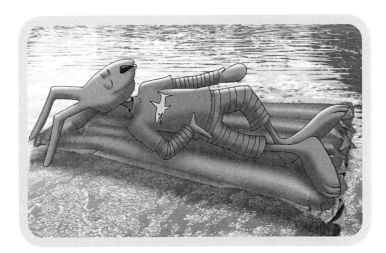

Free writing with picture cues. This page can also be used for sentence dictation using sentences from the book.

High-frequency words: the, is, he, has, to, for, a

Book 10d - Retell the story

'Mum Gets Strict'

This page can be photocopied onto card. Cut out these pictures for retelling the story or for children to make their own story. Can also be used to reinforce vocabulary.

Book 10d - Comprehension

Viv bumps into a box of plums.

Viv stamps and flaps her hands.

The plums land on top of Viv.

"Can I have crisps?" Viv begs.

Cut out the sentences. Read and match to the correct pictures.

Book 10d - Sentence dictation

to

a ____ of ____ .

Offer the sentence below as dictation. Encourage the children to sound out the words as they spell them.

Viv bumps in to a box of plums.

Book 10d - Sentence handwriting

Viv stamps and
flaps her hands.

Viv gets a hug
and a bag of
plums.

Handwriting practice for the key words for Book 10d.

Book 10d - Free writing

Free writing with picture cues. This page can also be used for sentence dictation using sentences from the book.

High-frequency words: I, have, no, is, her, to, a, of, the

Spelling list

print

crisps

stamp

stump

frogs

Frank

crust

twigs

slept

frost

A list of words from this Unit to be used for spelling practice.

Unit 10 - Game : ccvcc

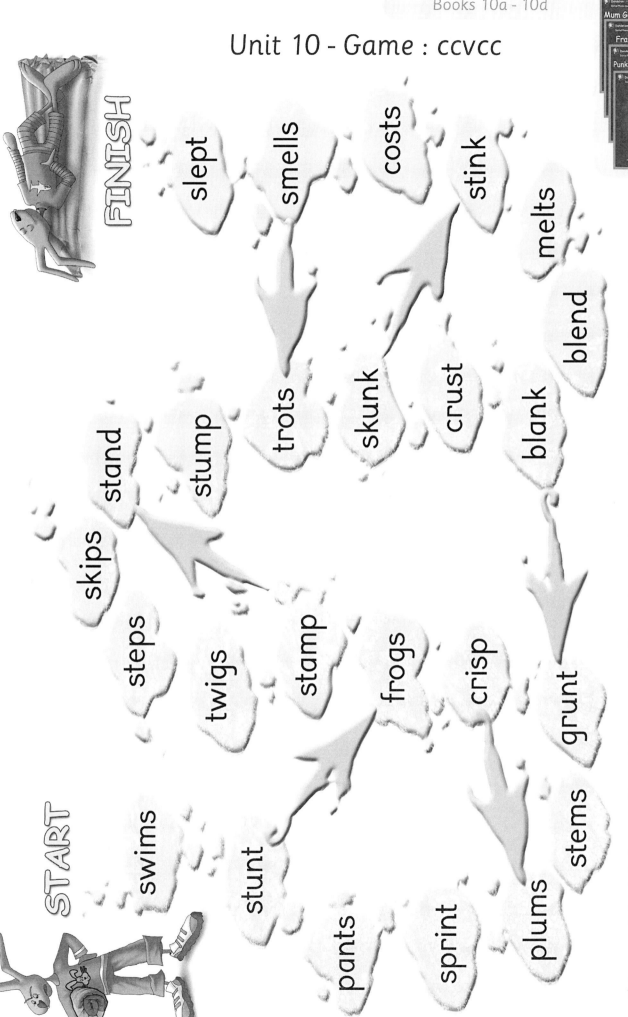

FINISH

START

slept

smells

costs

stink

melts

blend

trots

skunk

crust

blank

skips

stand

stump

steps

twigs

stamp

frogs

crisp

grunt

swims

stunt

pants

sprint

plums

stems

Mum Gets Strict
Frank Swims
Punk Smells Crisps
Stunt Rat

This game is for 1-4 players. Play with counters and die. Players take turns to throw the dice and move their counter.
Children read the word aloud as they land on it. Make sure the children use sounds rather than letter names.